Something Queer at the Ball Park

a mystery

YEARLING BOOKS/YOUNG YEARLINGS/YEARLING CLASSICS are designed especially to entertain and enlighten young people. Patricia Reilly Giff, consultant to this series, received her bachelor's degree from Marymount College and a master's degree in history from St. John's University. She holds a Professional Diploma in Reading and a Doctorate of Humane Letters from Hofstra University. She was a teacher and reading consultant for many years, and is the author of numerous books for young readers.

Something Queer at the Ball Park

a mystery

by
Elizabeth Levy
& illustrated by
Mordicai Gerstein

A Young Yearling Book

Published by
Dell Publishing
a division of
Bantam Doubleday Dell Publishing Group, Inc.
666 Fifth Avenue
New York, New York 10103

To George from Tommy
and
To Jesse and Aram from Summerstar

ISBN: 0-440-48116-3

Reprinted by arrangement with Delacorte Press

Printed in the United States of America

May 1984

10 9 8

CWO

A mysterious bearded figure stepped over Fletcher and knocked on Jill's back door.

Fletcher was Jill's dog. He opened one eye, but he didn't move. Fletcher almost never moved unless he had to.

The figure flashed a badge. "I just want to ask some questions," said the bearded person.

"Hey, Gwen, what do you want?" asked Jill.
"How did you know it was me?"
"You're the only kid who has a beard," said Jill.

GWEN! →

Gwen took off her beard and stuffed it back into her detective kit. "I'd like to watch you play baseball today," she said. "Are you ready to go?"

"Great," said Jill. "My dad just got me a new Rusty McGraw bat. I can't wait to use it."

CLOSE-UP OF JILL'S NEW RUSTY McGRAW BAT →

OFFICIAL
Rusty McGraw

Wham! Pow! With her new bat, Jill hit balls left and right. She was the star player of the Longfellow Raiders that day.

About a week later the coach gathered the team around him. "Our first game will be next Monday, on Memorial Day," said the coach, "and I'm going to announce the lineup just before game time."

COACH →

JILL ↓

After practice Jill said to Gwen, "Please help me look for my bat. I can't find it."

JILL FINDS A HALF EATEN PEANUT BUTTER SANDWICH. . . . BUT NO BAT

Gwen and Jill looked in Jill's locker, under all the benches, behind the water cooler. All over. No bat.

GWEN FINDS A NICKEL BUT NO BAT.

NO BAT HERE EITHE

(WHERE'S THAT BAT?)

Jill slammed her fist into her mitt. "It's my lucky bat. I'm no good without it."

(GENUINE "RUSTY McGRAW" MITT.)

The next day, Jill told the team that her Rusty McGraw bat was missing. She asked if anyone had seen it.

"Aw, Jill," said Ben, "that's your lucky bat. I hope you find it."

"Tough luck," said Marshall. "I never noticed it was a real Rusty McGraw bat."

"I didn't take it," said Erica.

Gwen stood outside the circle, tap, tap, tapping on her braces.

Gwen always tapped her braces whenever she thought something queer was going on. She put on one of her disguises.

Then, she snuck up behind Ben. She was trying to get a look at his bat. Ben turned around.

"What are you doing?" he asked.

"Oh, nothing," said Gwen. She crept away.

(GWEN, WEARING A BALD-WIG AND FALSE NOSE AND MOUSTACHE DISGUISE)

(GWEN, WEARING ANOTHER DISGUISE)

Next Gwen went up to Erica.

"Why did you tell the coach you didn't take Jill's bat?"

"Because I didn't," said Erica.

"Maybe," said Gwen. She walked away, tapping her braces.

A few minutes later, Gwen went up to Marshall.

"It seems funny you didn't know Jill's bat was a genuine Rusty McGraw," said Gwen.

"Why do you have on that funny-looking nose?" asked Marshall.

"Never mind," said Gwen.

← (YET ANOTHER DISGUISE)

On their way home, Gwen said to Jill, "Ben, Erica and Marshall were the only ones who said anything when you asked about your bat. I think one of them took it. I've been doing some detecting."

"I don't think anybody stole my bat," said Jill. "I probably left it someplace. Stay out of it, please. You'll only get me in trouble."

Jill was right. The next day, Erica said, "Your friend thinks I took your bat. I didn't, and I don't think she should say things that aren't true."

"Yeah," said Marshall. "She was sneaking around me, too. She's weird."

The coach came up to Jill. "I've heard rumors that someone thinks a team member stole your bat."

Jill shuffled her feet. "That's Gwen. She's my best friend."

"Tell her to stop bothering my team," the coach said. "A bat isn't that important. Just go out there and do your best."

As soon as Jill was alone, Gwen came running over. "I know a way to trap the kid who stole your bat."

"Oh, stop pretending to be a detective," cried Jill. "Nobody wants you snooping around."

"But . . . but . . ." sputtered Gwen.

"I'm sick of all your mysteries. This isn't a game. It's real. It's baseball."

Gwen stopped coming to the ballpark to watch Jill practice.

All week Jill tried every different bat the Longfellow Raiders had.

THE FIRST BAT

THE SECOND BAT

POP

She just couldn't hit the ball the way
she did with her Rusty McGraw bat.

Finally Jill went to see Gwen.

"I'm sorry for all the things I said."

"It's O.K.," said Gwen. "I knew you were upset. How's the baseball coming?"

"Awful," said Jill. "I've been in a real slump. Tomorrow's the first game, and I bet I'm not in the lineup."

"I still think somebody stole your bat, and I could find out who," said Gwen.

"I don't want to cause trouble," said Jill.

"But I have a great plan. I'll be out of sight. All we need is Fletcher and . . ." Gwen whispered her plan to Jill.

At practice the next morning, Jill walked around with a big smile. "I'm lucky to have my mitt," she said. "Maybe I lost my bat, but as long as I've got my mitt, I still feel lucky."

"That's the way to think," said the coach. "You're a dandy fielder. Don't worry about making the line-up. Just relax."

"Right," said Jill. "Just as long as I have my mitt."

Jill walked over to Fletcher.

"How're you doing, ole sleepy nose?" she asked. Jill scratched Fletcher on his belly. Fletcher lay on his back, waved his paws in the air, and grinned and grinned.

Jill got up and walked away. She had left her mitt beside Fletcher. It was a lovely day, and he fell asleep in the warm sun.

JILL'S MITT

Suddenly Fletcher's tail twitched. He
gave a yelp. He jumped up as if someone
had pulled his tail.

"It worked!!" shouted Gwen from behind the bushes. "Jill, come quick! Someone stole your mitt!"

Jill hopped on Gwen's bicycle. Gwen scooped up Fletcher and they took off.

They could just see the culprit round the corner on a bicycle.

"Whoever it is, is getting away!!" shouted Jill.

Gwen pedaled as fast as she could, but they couldn't catch up.

"I think it's a boy," said Gwen, "but I can't tell who."

THE CULPRIT

JILL'S MITT

JILL, GWEN + FLETCHER

"It's hopeless!" cried Jill. "Once he gets across Main Street, it's all downhill. We'll never catch up with this load."

Ahead of them they could hear music from a parade.

GRRRRRRRRR

Just as the boy reached Main Street, the parade rounded the corner. The boy hesitated. Gwen and Jill were almost on top of him. The band struck up, "Take Me Out to the Ballgame."

The boy tried to dash across the street in front of the parade.

Fletcher leapt out of the basket and sank his teeth into Jill's mitt, pulling the boy off his bike.

"It's Marshall!" screamed Jill.
"Get this dog off me!" cried Marshall. "He's heavy."
"Not until you tell where Jill's lucky bat is," said Gwen.

"O.K., O.K.," said Marshall. "I knew Jill was better than me. I thought that without her lucky bat, I'd have a good chance to make the lineup. When she said her mitt was lucky, I thought I'd better take that too."

"The mitt was a trap!" said Gwen. "Jill tied it to Fletcher's tail. She used invisible string from my detective kit."

"Now, where's my bat?" said Jill. "I need it."

"I'll show you," said Marshall. "Just get this dog off me."

Marshall took them to his house.
He had hidden the bat way in the
back of his closet.

"WHAT A MESS!" said Gwen.

"My bat!" cried Jill.

Fletcher lay down and started to chew
on one of Marshall's old sneakers.

They got Jill's bat and hurried back to the ball-park. The coach was so angry at Marshall that he didn't even let him play. Marshall had to be the water boy.

The coach picked Jill to play first base. She hit two home runs with her lucky Rusty McGraw bat.

Gwen and Fletcher sat in the grandstand and cheered every time it was Jill's turn.

JILL HITTING HER SECOND HOME WITH BASES LOADED ↙

← JILL MAKING A DIFFICULT CATCH IN THE 3RD INNING

LIZ →

Gwen kept twisting in her seat and looking around.

"What are you looking for?" asked Marshall as he came by carrying two buckets of water.

"You never can tell when something queer may happen," said Gwen, "... especially at a ballpark."